"What would happen if . . ."

A Look into a Cricket's Imagination and the Possibilities that Come with Creative Thinking

To Amanda Panda
Always use your
creative mind to lead you
on endless adventures!
All My Best
Christina Lafaro-Naclerio

CHRISTINA LAFARO-NACLERIO

AuthorHouse™
1663 Liberty Drive
Bloomington, IN 47403
www.authorhouse.com
Phone: 1 (800) 839-8640

Published by AuthorHouse 08/17/2017

ISBN: 978-1-5462-0457-2 (sc)
      978-1-5462-0458-9 (e)

Library of Congress Control Number: 2017912623

Print information available on the last page.

This book is printed on acid-free paper.

authorHOUSE®

Sebastian, Your inquisitive mind inspires me.

What would happen if the grass grew all the way up to the sky?

Would worms grow wings and learn to fly?

2

3

What would happen if school was at night and bedtime during the day?

Would you need a flash light to go out and play?

What would happen if your bathtub was full of lemon jello?

After your bath, would your body be yellow?

What would happen if as you got older your body grew small?

Would you be able to walk or maybe just crawl?

8

What would happen if you ate broccoli for dessert and candy for dinner?

Would your belly get big or maybe get thinner?

10

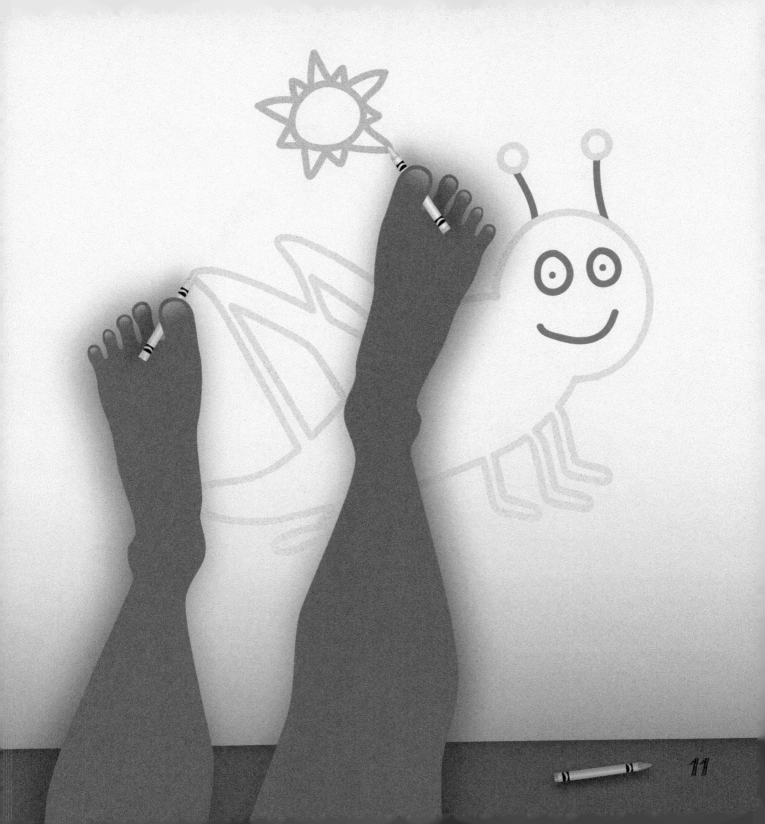

What would happen if you ate with your eyes and saw with your nose?

Would you talk with your hands and write with your toes?

What would happen if pizza was cold and ice cream was hot?

Would you still like to eat them...
not at all,
or a lot?

15

What would happen if Mommy let you pick out your own clothes to wear?

Would you remember to put on your underwear?

What would happen if you brushed your hair with a fork and you ate with your brush?

Would your hair look neat or would it be covered in mush?

19

What would happen if in the middle of school you heard someone fart?

Would you giggle and point or try to act smart?

These are the things I think of each day...
When I use my brain in my own Special way.

Christina Lafaro-Naclerio was born and raised in Eastchester, NY and is currently residing in White Plains, NY. She studied Elementary Education and has specialized in the Special Education field for over 25 years. Her dedication to opening the minds of children and the inspiration of her Mother, who was a very talented author and artist before her passing, have led to her new passion for writing. This is her first published book and will be the start of a series of "What would happen if?" books to follow.

Danielle Ciccotelli is a full time Graphic Designer at Dobbs Creative Group, LLC. in Sparta, NJ. "What would happen if?" is her first published book as illustrator and she is very excited to continue the series along side cousin Christina.

Photo taken by Linda Bernadic

CPSIA information can be obtained
at www.ICGtesting.com
Printed in the USA
BVOW05s1800040917

493820BV00006B/6/P

9 781546 204572